NORMAN BRIDWELL

Clifford
AND THE BIG STORM

SCHOLASTIC INC.
New York Toronto London Auckland Sydney

For Diana and Michael Norton

ISBN 0-590-25755-2

12   8 9/9 0/0

Printed in the U.S.A.   24

First Scholastic printing, April 1995
Colorist: Manny Campana

Hi! I'm Emily Elizabeth.
Have you met my dog, Clifford?
We have some exciting adventures together.
Last summer he took me to the seashore
to visit my grandma.

Clifford loves the ocean.

It's big enough for him to swim in.

He watched my friends and me
build castles in the sand.

Clifford built one, too.

Then we wanted to go fishing.
There was no room for us on the pier....

But that didn't matter,
because we had Clifford!

One day we couldn't go swimming or fishing.
We heard that a big storm was coming up the coast.

The police told everybody along the shore to leave
for a safer place.

Grandma hated to leave her little home.

Clifford took us away from the beach
to a high school gym.

We were safe there. But Clifford knew that
Grandma was worried about her house.

He hurried back to the beach.
The wind and rain could not stop him.

The storm was bad. Trees were falling down.

Big waves were crashing up on the shore.
Grandma's house was in danger.

Clifford had to do something!
First he picked up some of the fallen trees.

He piled the trees in back of Grandma's house
and covered them with sand.
The sand pile would block the waves.

While Clifford was packing down the sand,
he saw a bolt of lightning hit the lighthouse!

The lighthouse began to burn.
Clifford knew just what to do.

Whoosh! The fire was out.

Then, over the roar of the storm,
Clifford heard another sound.
It was two puppies. They were scared!

Clifford reached the puppies just in time.

He made sure his new friends were safe.
Then he ran back to Grandma's.

Oh, oh! There was more trouble.

Two boats were loose in the waves.

They were about to crash!

Clifford brought them safely ashore.

The waves kept getting bigger.

Clifford was afraid the sand pile would be washed away.

He lay down to guard the house. What would happen next?

The storm kept blowing all night.
We wondered where Clifford was.

The next morning the police said we could go back to Grandma's.

Her house was safe behind a big pile of sand.

But we didn't see Clifford anywhere.

Surprise!

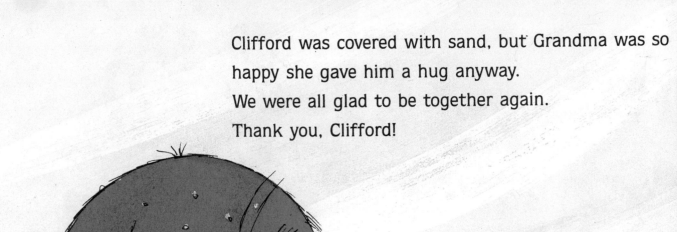

Clifford was covered with sand, but Grandma was so
happy she gave him a hug anyway.
We were all glad to be together again.
Thank you, Clifford!